Mishaps of the Heart

The tales and short stories of love lost and found

By : S Dabon

Studio of Books LLC
5900 Balcones Drive Suite 100
Austin, Texas 78731
www.studioofbooks.org
Hotline: (254) 800-1183

Ordering Information:
Special discounts are available on quantity purchases by corporations, associations, and others. For details, contact the publisher at the address above.

Printed in the United States of America.

ISBN-13: Softcover   979-8-9900465-1-1
          eBook   978-1-964148-14-4

Library of Congress Control Number: 2024906611

CONTENTS

DEDICATION

To Liam and Mae, who opened the doors for me to finally become an author after a decade of shelving my stories and losing hope of ever giving this book the light of day.

To Hanna Marionne, the first person I ever shared my stories with, and helped me edit them since who else should read and edit them but a best friend who does editing for a living?

To the inspiration of these stories, who I doubt will buy and read them. Thanks anyway.

To the love of my life, Nikko. You are my anchor. Thank you for always feeding me when I am "hangry".

Lastly and more importantly, to Summer and Autumn. I love you girls more than you can imagine. May this inspire you to be creative when you grow up and forgive mommy for giving you really long names.

MIA AND RAYMOND - THE INEVITABLE

"My world has become different. Even with the thought of you, I will remain in the shadows."

I stare back at him, wide eyed and entranced. I try to absorb everything he has said recently, although we've been looking at each other for quite a long time.

"I don't understand. Why now?" I ask him silently, without missing a beat. I can sense that he's tense, staring down at his hands as if looking for a response that will help make the issue at hand less alarming.

"Babe, this is really a big opportunity for me."

"You told me you wouldn't go."

He looks at me exasperatingly.

"It's not as easy as you think Mia."

His eyes narrow and his lips are pressed into a thin line. I know deep inside he's mad. Mad at me for being too pessimistic, too close minded that this relationship will work despite the distance. But in his eyes, I know he's more frustrated, knowing that he would need to choose between me and his career. I fight back the urge to cry, I will not tear up in front of him, not when he's just inches away from me, vulnerable and pleading.

"Don't make it more difficult than it already is."

"I'm not making things hard for you Raymond." I sigh. I wasn't aware that I was holding my breath until then. I tear my eyes away from him.

I couldn't bear his presence, let alone stare at him when we know what's about to happen.

"You promised to stay no matter what, just like I did when you needed me the most. I kept my end of the promise, but it seems like you've made up your mind."

I can feel him looking at me but I hear no response. He lets out an exasperated garble. But I don't think he's giving me any sensible reply. I clench my fists tighter. My nails are burying into my flesh and they're starting to hurt and sting, but not as much as the sting and pain I'm feeling in my chest. A threatening silence envelopes us, and I knew right then that once one of us speaks, everything will be over.

I take a step towards the door and he looks up. He stares at me, tears threatening to fall from his eyes. I look at him as I try to suppress a sob. He reaches for me but I take a step back. "No." I say, voice cracking.

"Mia I..."

"No. Don't say or do anything that 'll make me stay. It won't help."

He looks at me stunned. He stands up but keeps his distance, face unsure of what to do to keep me from leaving.

"There are so many decisions and mistakes we have to make in this world Mia." He says quietly, as his breathing hollows.

"Well sometimes you make one wrong decision, and you'll realize that's the only opportunity you had, and you'll never have it back."

I look at him one last time and he's still as handsome as ever. His boyish looks and piercing eyes that seem to lose their soul with each teardrop and second that has made us fall apart. I wish to wash away all the worries and pain he has and bring back the life his face once had. I recall the memories of our first conversation at the beach, the little grin he had when he reached out his hand and helped me to get up after falling flat on the sand. Those were the good days. The days when love was more irresistible than fame and fortune. When love was enough to keep us sated and satisfied. Yes, love was all that mattered.

I shake myself awake, and drive away all the memories at the back of my mind. I return to the man I know now. Eyes wary and seeking, he deems for more than just love to exist. I sigh one more time and he glances at me, yearning, trying to prolong what's about to be done.

I feel the urge to kiss him and take all our inhibitions away. But my mind gets the best of me and gingerly, I open the door out of our apartment.

"Goodbye Raymond."

MIA AND RAYMOND - THE CRACKS THAT WERE LEFT OPEN

"And in our efforts to keep the peace, we fall into pieces."

It's 6am and the sun is glaring outside my window. I swipe the curtains away as I take in the heat inside my bedroom. It's been three months since the last time we saw each other. Yet I feel my heart twitch at the mere thought of him. Yes, he still has that effect on me. Raymond. My Raymond… or was.

Lifelessly, I sit at the end of the bed. I close my eyes and let the memories of him fill my entire being. I remember the last night I was in his apartment. I shiver as I recall the deafening silence that was followed by the ear shattering words I spoke when I left. "Goodbye Raymond."

I sigh. Earlier that day our morning was full of excitement and anticipation for what we had set out to accomplish. We were discussing possible companies I could work for now that I've graduated.

"Have you considered Kingston?" Raymond says between mouthfuls of scrambled eggs. He sits himself near the kitchen counter, his free hand idly tapping his bottle of orange juice.

I smile at him tentatively as I fiddle with my food. "Hmmm. Kingston's a big advertising company Ray. I'm not sure I'll fit in."

"Babe please, you're the smartest person I know."

I pout. "That doesn't exactly give me merit."

He laughs. That boyish and heartfelt laugh he always had when he's amused. I arch an eyebrow at him and he smirks.

"Trust me Mia, you'll do good in Kingston."

He takes my free hand and kisses it gently as he gives me a reassuring squeeze. I give in for a moment to his sweet little gesture.

"But Kingston's quite far from home don't you think?"

He stirs and I glance at him. He grows tense under my scrutiny and I can sense that something's wrong.

"Babe?" I ask, confusion blatant in my burrowed eyebrows.

"It's not that far Mia." He answers quietly, his eyes not meeting mine. "Besides, we'll need to move away from Delaware eventually."

"Move... eventually?" I look at him perplexed. I release my hand from his grip and he looks up , startled. I give him a gawking look but he doesn't answer.

"Is there something you'd like to tell me, Raymond?" I ask, observing every move he makes. His mouth twitches, a sign that he's nervous or anxious about something. He sighs audibly and shrugs.

"Babe, let's talk about this when I get home after work. I need to get to the studio now."

I gaze at him intently, not ready to back down from this conversation. I want to sort things out NOW. I hold his right arm loosely and tug him to look at me, I stare at him questioningly.

He looks at me nervous. "Mia, please. You have four interviews today and they're pretty far away. Let's not ruin your mood. Today's a big day."

I released him from my grip and focused on my food. I knew something big was about to happen. But I never would have guessed what was about to happen next.

UNFULFILLED PROMISES 1

BURDEN.

She lights up another cigarette as her last puff fades into the air. She's been awake for hours now, nestling with only three hours of sleep in a day. This has been her routine for the past few weeks; waking up in the middle of a tiring day at work, and not being able to go back to sleep. She says to everyone that asks that she's stressed out because of her job. But those who really knew her know better.

"I'm starting to be a little blurry to him."

"Shut up, no one asked you."

The orange fur ball purred.

"You don't have to be so upset, love. Isn't this what you wanted?"

He sits right next to her, waving his tail in one of her calves and giving a sly smile.

"You know, for a talking cat you're too annoying."

"You don't have a choice."

"You'll be gone soon you know."

The cat gives her a sad look.

"I know. I'm just not sure if this is something good for you. You've been suppressing me all these weeks and I don't think it's making you any better."

She gives out a little laugh and decides to pet the furry animal next to her.

"This is helping him."

"And you? What about you?"

"I don't know." She sighs. She lights up another cigarette and puffs it a little faster this time. She looks away and pretends to puff some more so the cat doesn't see her tears.

"I really don't understand why you're here."

"We both know you do." The orange feline moves towards her and looks at her directly in the eye.

"I am the mutual love between you and him. You can see me and so does he. But the moment one of you stops fighting for that love, I will leave. And you will never see me again."

She takes the cat and places it on her arms. She hugs her tight, holding on to him like he was her lifeline. It was beautiful and painful to watch.

"I will miss you, cat."

"Does this mean…"

"This isn't about not fighting for it." She answers, her voice mumbling in the empty room. The cat sets himself free from her embrace and sits near her window.

"He has made a choice. No matter how much I fight for it, there's no use. You can't win a losing battle Cat, let alone fight for something only you believe in. I can take all the pain and bruises, as long as I know both of us still believe in you, but that's the problem, only I do. Only I believe in you. He doesn't. I don't think he ever did."

The cat stands up and glances at her.

"There's a reason why you still see me and though I am blurry to him, he sees me too. You may be in a losing battle, but the choice to fight and give it all you have is yours. At least assure me you won't leave any tables unturned when you both decide to get rid of me. The world can only handle so many people with regrets for not being bold enough to give it their all, don't be one of them."

And with that, he vanishes into thin air. She stares at the spot where the orange cat last lingered. She sighs, unsure of what she should feel with his last words. She closes her windows and lights up another cigarette. This time, she's not sure whether she'd see the cat in her room again.

A BEAT.

He stares blankly at the screen of his phone as he reads her message. A phrase, a sentence of some sort that held so many questions he does not want to be answered. He keeps blinking, as if detaching himself from the words she has said. *"Please, we really need to talk."*

He tosses the phone in the bed and tries to make some sense of what he just read. Her message sounded so pleading, desperate even. He could only imagine how much courage it took her to send those words let alone type them. He felt the urge to call her but then stopped himself when he realized he wasn't alone.

"Babe, are you okay?"

"Hmm?"

"You seem a little distracted. Is everything alright?"

"Yeah, I just feel a bit under the weather, but I'll be fine."

"Okay. I have to go now. I'll see you after work."

She kisses him on the cheek and hugs him tight. He feels a pang of guilt for lying to her again, but he couldn't bring to tell her about the real reason for his distraction. He takes her to the doorstep and gives her a small wave as he closes the door behind her.

He goes back up to his room and takes the phone in hands. He couldn't afford to make the same mistake again. He already did. They already did. He types the best excuse he could come up with and presses send before he can change his mind. As the screen shows "message sent" he releases a huge sigh and tosses the phone back on the bed. He knows the reply is going to hurt her more than ever, but this is what he has to do. This is what's best for them, and somehow he wants to convince himself that this is the best for her too.

He sits at the edge of the bed, head buried in his hands. He feels a headache coming, a kind of headache no medication can fix. He knows she won't be sleeping much after she's read his message, and the thought of stressing her out makes him worried and anxious. He remembers the days when everything was so easy for them; when he was the reason for her smiles, not her tears; when he was her inspiration, not her distraction; when she sings songs of love and dreams, not of heartaches and broken promises. She was at her best, in her element, she was in love. But he was not.

He finally flops in bed in the hope of getting some rest, when a familiar orange feline appears near his side lamp, purring constantly as he moves closer to the edge of his bed.

"Cat?"

"You can still see me. That's something."

He ignores the other's sarcasm. "How is she?"

"Not as strong as you suppose."

He stills; a twitch of pain apparent in his eyes. Cat senses this and tries to explain further.

"She pleaded to see you and talk to you. And you replied by saying you can't because you were with a different woman. You don't expect her to be fine, do you?"

He looks away and Cat continues.

"You miss her."

"Yes. I do."

"Then meet her."

"You know I can't do that." He says, his eyes full of desperation. He looks up, trying to fight the urge to cry.

"Then let her go if you can't be with her."

"You know I can't do that either."

"That's very selfish of you." The orange fur ball says as he walks towards the other edge of his bed.

"This person is willing to give up everything for you and now you choose not to be with her. But you also do not want to let her go. How do you reconcile that? How will she move on if you're still giving her false hopes? You're giving her crumbs and pieces but she still accepts them like they're big enough to create good memories of you. Do you really think she deserves to be treated this way?"

He sighs audibly and buries his head in his hands again. The confusion he feels is relentless and he doesn't know what to think or do. He knows the cat is right, he has to set her free, and has to talk to her about it. But he doesn't have the courage to do so. He's a coward, he knows. He knows that at some point they'll have to part, but the thought of losing her completely is something he does not want to think about.

"You can't avoid the inevitable. Think about it. And before yourself, think about her." The cat waves its tail in his direction and disappears into thin air, leaving him behind.

FIRST OF MANY FAREWELLS AND A LITTLE EUPHORIA ON WHAT MIGHT HAVE BEEN.

"The greatest coward is a man who awakens a woman's love with no intention of loving her." –Bob Marley

He sees her in the corner of his eye and although he tries hard to look away, he ends up staring at her. She moves swiftly across the room towards her seat, hastily placing her essentials on her table. Unconscious of the sad look he gives her.

"Weird." He thinks. She seems unencumbered by the fact that they were the only ones in the office so early. He feels a pang of pain in his chest that he tries to dismiss, but it only grows stronger as she smiles towards another person who greets her as he passes.

He decides to ignore it. But his mind doesn't seem to cooperate with him today, as it takes a mental note of every action she makes. *Everything that does not involve him.* He makes a resolve to at least clear his mind with thoughts of her when he meets his girlfriend later that day. She doesn't have to know that another woman is running through his mind.

He idly goes through his tasks and decides to work on them even if he still has fifteen minutes before work actually starts. He thinks, if he immerses himself with too much workload he'll forget the thought that she has forgotten about him. It worked for about a minute, when he tried hard. But who was he kidding? Who can go on forgetting someone who has been on your mind for the last few days, and having her in such close proximity; only a very determined jerk could do that. And then he remembers her last message to him that said those exact words. He laughs inwardly at the irony of his situation. "Isn't this what you wanted? For her to forget about you and move on with her life like she always has, just without you in the picture?" He massages his temples and closes his eyes.

"Ah. Fuck logic." he murmurs.

Lunch break comes and he gets a glimpse of her laughing about an email her seatmate has just sent. He was too far to see what the email was about but he heard her say something about why people should date a woman who reads. He gets that. She loves to read, and write. Those were just a few of the things he admired about her. Her way with words and the ability to see beauty in every piece she reads made her different from all the others he has ever known.

He remembers the gifts she gave him a month back: A book from one of her favorite writers and a journal. He remembers her little ramble about how he never had the time to buy his own damn notebook and she thought he was just being lazy so she, as a frustrated writer, desperately had to buy him one. He had laughed at her then, saying she thought too much about what to give him when he in return only gave her a journal. The comment made her frown, and he smiled at her and said the only words he could fathom. "Thank you." She smiled a little, and went on mumbling about how he should start reading the book she gave and "You should really use that journal since you clearly pointed out that it's more expensive than what you got me."

He grinned as she walked away from him then. He will never forget that day. It was the day she first said goodbye.

UNFULFILLED PROMISES 2

(The Last of the few reasons to write about uncertainties)

TAINTED.

She purses her lips and holds back the nudging feeling to hold his hand as he sits across her. She clasps her own hands tight, waiting for him to be well settled as silence envelopes the uncertainty of what this meeting could bring.

She has imagined it before: Him sitting right next to her, holding her hand, pleading her not to go. Begging for her to realize that everything about them was true. And that he cared so much for her to be mad, so mad that she could leave without hurting him. "I love you." The dream said. "I love you beyond time and life itself."

But here they are: in a cramped, cold place, across each other, not breathing a single word.

He looks at her expectantly and she meets his eye. For a moment they looked at each other in an attempt to encourage the other to talk first. She looks away and he sighs, breaking the quiet tension between them.

"So, what do you plan to do after you go?"

She hesitates, and drinks a little from the bottle of pink juice in her hand. This was not the conversation she had hoped for. Yet, at the back of her mind she realized this was something she expected. Yes, expected.

Her mind however, altered and clouded her thoughts with too much faith and hope that should have long been crushed.

"Rest. Go places I guess."

"I'm planning to study again."

She looks up and meets his gaze. And for the first time in a long while, she smiles.

"Really? Wow. What are you planning to take up? Where do you want to go to school?"

He gives her the details of his plans and when he thinks he can do it. He tells her with ease and so much enthusiasm that she remembers the last time they talked about something similar to this. A few days back, she told him about her plans of going to law school and how she envied her friends for having the resources to study.

"If only I had the money, I would have been taking my masters or law school now. But hey, dreams take time right?"

She remembers him laughing at her and rambling about how he disliked the degree he took. How he wished he took something else: Something he was passionate for like she did.

Now, she sees him incoherently talking about taking up a masters degree and how no one stays in the current job they have for very long. Somehow, she wants to believe she has inspired him. But she dismisses the thought as it entails other emotions she does not want to surface.

The conversation took different turns as it involved everyone else… *except them*. They talked about cars, gossip in the office, work ethics, who got sacked, who's about to get sacked, who lost weight and who's avoiding who. They managed to avoid the very reason why they even decided to be alone in the first place, and yet no one dared to sail into that direction.

He continues his rant on a disappointing colleague who he thinks lacks work values. She nods, only half- listening to his so-called observations.

"I mean, if you're not cut out for it, you shouldn't take it out on anyone."

She quirks an eyebrow.

"What do you mean?"

"I'm saying, he shouldn't be too emotional and take it out on other people when he's pissed."

She rolls her eyes.

"What?"

"You're emotional to me when you're pissed."

"I'm talking about professional stuff." He reasons. "What we have is different. We're personally involved with each other."

"Hmm…"

He cuts the conversation off and they walk back towards the parking lot. He continues to talk about certain plans and things he has to do. She nonchalantly nods at him, preoccupied with her own thoughts.

This is it. She thinks.

This was their last talk. Their last everything. After this, she will cut all ties and do her best to never see him again. She stops walking and he notices, walking back to where she decided to halt.

"What's wrong?"

"Nothing. I think I'm going to walk from here."

"You're not going back to the office?"

"No. I'm heading home."

"Okay." He looks at her questioningly and continues to walk on. "I need to get back now."

"I know."

For a moment, she thought she couldn't do it. She was stuck between doing what she wanted and what she hoped for and what she expected and… - she is just confused.

"Ah. Fuck Logic." She thinks.

She signals him to come closer and when he is close enough, she hugs him. It wasn't what she wanted or hoped. But it was not something she expected either. She did what she felt was right. And in this feeling of sadness and bliss, she breaks away and holds his hand for the last time.

She longed and ached for this moment: this touch, for the warmth they once shared, and for the rush they once brought.

It was then that she found out, those moments when a few seconds seem like forever… They only happen in movies. He lets go, and from that instant she knows everything about them will be nothing but memories.

Memories she will soon forget, bury, and lock somewhere far where she can never reach them.

They walk in different routes and she hears him call her one last time.

"We're still going to live in the same city you know."

"I know."

"I'm just here. We're going to see each other."

She waves him goodbye and starts walking away opposite his direction. When he disappears into the building, she pauses and breathes in deeply. She drank the last of her pink juice and held the bottle idly in her hand. While resting, something familiar caught her eye. A car was parked right where she decided to stop. "It's Penguin." She says, recognizing the car immediately as she reads the plate. She lingers for a moment and recalls his last words to her.

"We're going to see each other."

She shakes her head with the thought of seeing him again. She looks at her empty bottle, and remembers he bought it for her today. She walks towards the car and places the empty bottle on the trunk lid.

"See each other? **YOU WISH**."

THE AFTERMATH: AN EPILOGUE OF SORTS

"Letting go is madness, but it sets you free."

STUPOR.

He holds her hand and their fingers intertwine. I see her laughing and giving him a slight touch in the arm.

Tragic.

So tragically familiar.

I keep a good distance behind the flood of people who seem to find comfort in crowding the streets of the city today. I was on my way to meet a couple of old friends when someone familiar caught my eye.

I should say: her long brown hair shines gracefully with the sun. She has become supple like that of a new tree that bore its first fruit. Her crunched forehead looks more adorable as it had ever been. Her bright eyes and silent lips glisten when she hastily flips the next page of her new book. Ah… a book, as always. The innate bookworm in her never seizes to amaze me. And yet I could not say any of these words to her. Not to anyone. Such a waste.

Yes it is awful. So awfully true.

I contemplate on whether I should muster all the confidence and courage to talk to her. Yet even at the thought of being in such close proximity with her nauseates me. And for some unfathomable reason, I have an odd hint that the feeling is mutual.

I keep my earphones on and distract myself with the rest of the people passing by. They seem to become fewer now, and my fear of being seen by her has grown a little stronger. Edgy, I walk in and settle a few tables behind her, luckily finding a newspaper that seems to have lost its purpose for its previous owner. I hid my face from view, and I stared with content on the mirror behind her.

Stalking.

Creepy.

What a waste of time and effort.

And yet I couldn't stop myself from doing it.

Not for her anyway.

Her phone rings and she's taken away from her book daze. She smiles widely as she looks at the name reflected on her screen. That smile. The smile that used to give me flutters in the stomach and would always keep me light headed. That candid smile she gives whenever I give her a new song to listen to, or whenever I crack jokes that only she can get, or when we describe and say what we like and we always end up liking the same things.

I used to make her smile like that.

That's right. Used to.

And now, I'm the one in a daze.

He surprises her from behind, with a bouquet of white and blue roses. I chuckle, such a cliché. Then my heart aches a little as I remember how she painstakingly reiterated her love for flowers to me. Yes. For blue and white roses to be exact.

Her face lights up and she gives him the most beautiful smile I have ever seen. Something she has given me once before. And yet the happiness she resonates now is way more endearing, more genuine. Even if I combine all my days, weeks and months with her, they will not suffice nor contest with the blissful and contented face of the woman in front of me.

A part of me wants to leave them and go to my friends as planned. But my legs are glued to the ground and I am entranced. This version of her: this happy and in love version of her is something I have not seen.

No wait.

I have seen this before.

But she wasn't happy and in love with him.

She was in love with ME.

I keep my head down as she gives him a kiss on the cheek and he responds by teasing her to kiss him on the lips. She acts annoyed but they both knew she was only being playful. He grabs her bag and her carefully laid book from the table, not forgetting the bookmark so she can get back to the last page she was reading before he came. Great, even the part about the bookmark is something he knows.

My gaze trails them as they leave the coffee shop and hail a cab. I hear them bickering about what movie to watch and they resolve it by saying he gets to choose only if he doesn't talk when the film starts. He laughs and kisses her on the forehead and whispers the words I never had the audacity to say.

"I love you."

She smiles and whispers back.

"I love you too."

Their cab leaves and my eyes follow them until they become little dots and disappear from view.

Something inside me shatters a little. No. More than a little.

Then the rain begins to pour.

How overly dramatic.

And perfect for this infinitely definite moment.

THE CAT'S FAREWELL

*"Some goodbyes are worthy of a celebration. They
emancipate you from your chains."*

"I'm surprised to see you again."

She says smiling as the feline across her snorts. It purrs once and then lies next to her.

"Let's just say I'm here for a special occasion."

"Hmm."

"Why do I feel like I'm not welcome?"

She laughs whole-heartedly and pats the cat slightly. She carries it into her lap and pets her gently.

"Oh you are Cat. It's what you represent that's not welcome."

"Hmm."

She lays it back in bed and moves towards her side table to grab her phone. She taps on a few buttons and puts the screen in front of the cat's face.

"See that? He has my heart now you know."

It glances at the screen and looks right back at her.

"Do you love him?"

She smiles genuinely. "Yes."

"He obviously loves you more than you love him."

She rolls her eyes.

"I know."

"No wonder your new cat hasn't showed up yet."

"I don't think I will need a cat this time."

"Do you plan to destroy all of us and make us go extinct?"

She laughs and carries the orange feline in her arms. She hugs it tightly and breathes long before speaking.

"I just think…" she pauses.

"Maybe this time I don't need anyone else to remind me that there's mutual love between me and who I'm with. The truth is, I feel it every day. He makes it known and felt, so the fear of uncertainties doesn't haunt me anymore. I'm not afraid to be seen with him, I'm even proud. And the feeling is overwhelmingly mutual."

She places her right hand on her chest and smiles.

"I guess this wandering heart has finally found its home."

The cat stares at her momentarily and moves away subtly from her grasp.

"You've finally found a way to live without me."

"I guess so."

"Then I suppose this is goodbye."

They both smile.

"Will you tell him?"

She asks as she opens the window for the orange furball. It seems confused with her question so she tries again.

"The other half of you, the other person who can see you, will you tell him?"

The cat leaps gracefully and faces her.

"There's no need to tell him anything, love. Trust me, he already knows."

And with that, the feline leaves and disappears from her view forever.

GRIEF: PICKING THE FRAGMENTS OF YOUR SOUL

"Grief is the last act of love we have to give to those we love. Where there is deep grief, there was deep love."- Anonymous

It starts with a small crack.

It begins with her eating in one of his favorite restaurants. She orders for two and realizes a little too late that she no longer has anyone to share it with.

Her lips quiver, but she bites it to keep herself from falling apart in front of a total stranger.

"Fuck..." she utters.

The cashier gives her a reassuring smile but she pushes through with the order with no intention of eating the extra sundae.

~ ~ ~ ~ ~

"How do you deal with grief?" She asks with puffy eyes and clogged nostrils. It was just hours before he passed and she was in such a state of stupor she barely remembers how she met with six people who all gave her concerned looks.

"Can you eat something first, please?"

She gives them a blank stare.

She has no idea what to do.

~ ~ ~ ~

And the pieces begin to break.

A new film he liked is showing soon and she chances at a poster of the movie. She wants to watch it but fear overcomes her. Tears threaten to fall from her eyes and she leaves before anyone notices.

~ ~ ~ ~

"You seem to be taking this lightly." One comments as she continuously encodes her report. Her fingers are still vigorously tapping the keys as she quirks an eyebrow and the other one continues.

"He was just buried yesterday, right? I'm just surprised to see you working today."

She stills.

"I need to work." she says, stressing every syllable without looking up. The other one gives her a stunned look at the sentiment and leaves without missing a beat. Those four words are what it took so no one would bother her for the rest of the day.

~ ~ ~ ~ ~ ~ ~ ~

And then the final piece.

She wakes up with a stir and she hears her mom knocking on her door.

"Hey, something was delivered for you."

Her excitement builds up as she dresses up and hastens. She washes her face and fixes her hair in a lopsided bun since she was in a hurry.

Just then, the most beautiful bouquet of white roses greets her eyes as she runs down the staircase.

"Oh my god, I love them!" she exclaims, and she brings it upstairs to thank her closest friend for remembering.

By this time, the crack has inevitably shattered her heart to pieces.

A tear.

A cry of sadness.

At last, she has embraced grief.

And for a long time she was running. Now, she finally has the courage to write the words she should have written a long time ago:

~ ~ ~ ~

My love,

Sadness does not even come close to how I feel about you. It just doesn't seem fair for you to leave me the way you did.

I am hurt... and I am in so much pain.

I lost you.

And there's no way to have you back.

Sometimes I blame myself, thinking I could have done more to save you, to prolong your life, to spend more time with you when I could. And it breaks me everyday because I can no longer do that. Tell me, how is it even possible for someone to continuously break you even when they've left you behind?

I love and hate you.

You always remembered how I love receiving flowers no matter what. Yet you hate bringing them because you don't want people to know you're a sap.

Or how you hate vegetables but you eat it so mama won't think you hate her cooking.

Or that you hate reading but you buy books for me because you know I'm a bookworm.

And I can go on all day with stories about you. God knows I would if that can bring you back. It's just that it wouldn't. But if this random use of words could tell you something, it should only tell you this.

I miss you.

I love you.

Beyond measure.

Beyond the soul and love itself.

And hopefully in time, I can put the pieces of who I am back again.

Until then...

www.ingramcontent.com/pod-product-compliance
Lightning Source LLC
Chambersburg PA
CBHW061553310726
48972CB00008B/2743